I DIDN'T STAND UP

WRITTEN BY
Lucy Falcone

ILLUSTRATED BY
Jacqueline Hudon

CLOCKWISE
PRESS

Published by Clockwise Press Inc., 42 Sunbird Blvd, Keswick ON L4P 3R9

solange@clockwisepress.com
www.clockwisepress.com
10 9 8 7 6 5 4 3 2 1

Library and Archives Canada Cataloguing in Publication

Falcone, L. M. (Lucy M.), 1951-, author
I didn't stand up / written by Lucy Falcone ;
illustrated by Jacqueline Hudon.
A poem.

ISBN 978-1-988347-06-6 (hardcover)

I. Hudon, Jacqueline, illustrator II. Title. III. Title: I did not stand up.
PS8561.A574I2 2018   jC811'.6   C2018-905387-9

Data available on file
Design by Jacqueline Hudon
Printed in Canada by Friesens

Canada Council Conseil des arts
for the Arts   du Canada

We acknowledge the support of the Canada Council for the Arts, which last year invested $153 million to bring the arts to Canadians throughout the country.
Nous remercions le Conseil des arts du Canada de son soutien. L'an dernier, le Conseil a investi 153 millions de dollars pour mettre de l'art dans la vie des
Canadiennes et des Canadiens de tout le pays.

This book is dedicated to all children
who are suffering at the hands of bullies.

- LF

For Félix. I hope you stand up.

- JH

First they went after Jamal.

But I'm not black —

so I didn't stand up for him.

Then they went after Duncan.

But I'm not a geek –

So I didn't stand up for him.

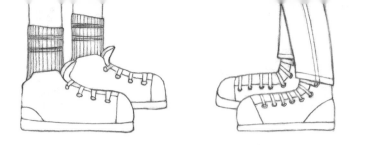

Then they went after Shyanne.
But my clothes aren't hand-me-downs –
So I didn't stand up for her.

Then they went after Mariana.
But I was born in this country –
So I didn't stand up for her.

Then they went after Jason.
But I'm not gay –
So I didn't stand up for him.

Then they went after Aisha.
But I'm not Muslim —
So I didn't stand up for her.

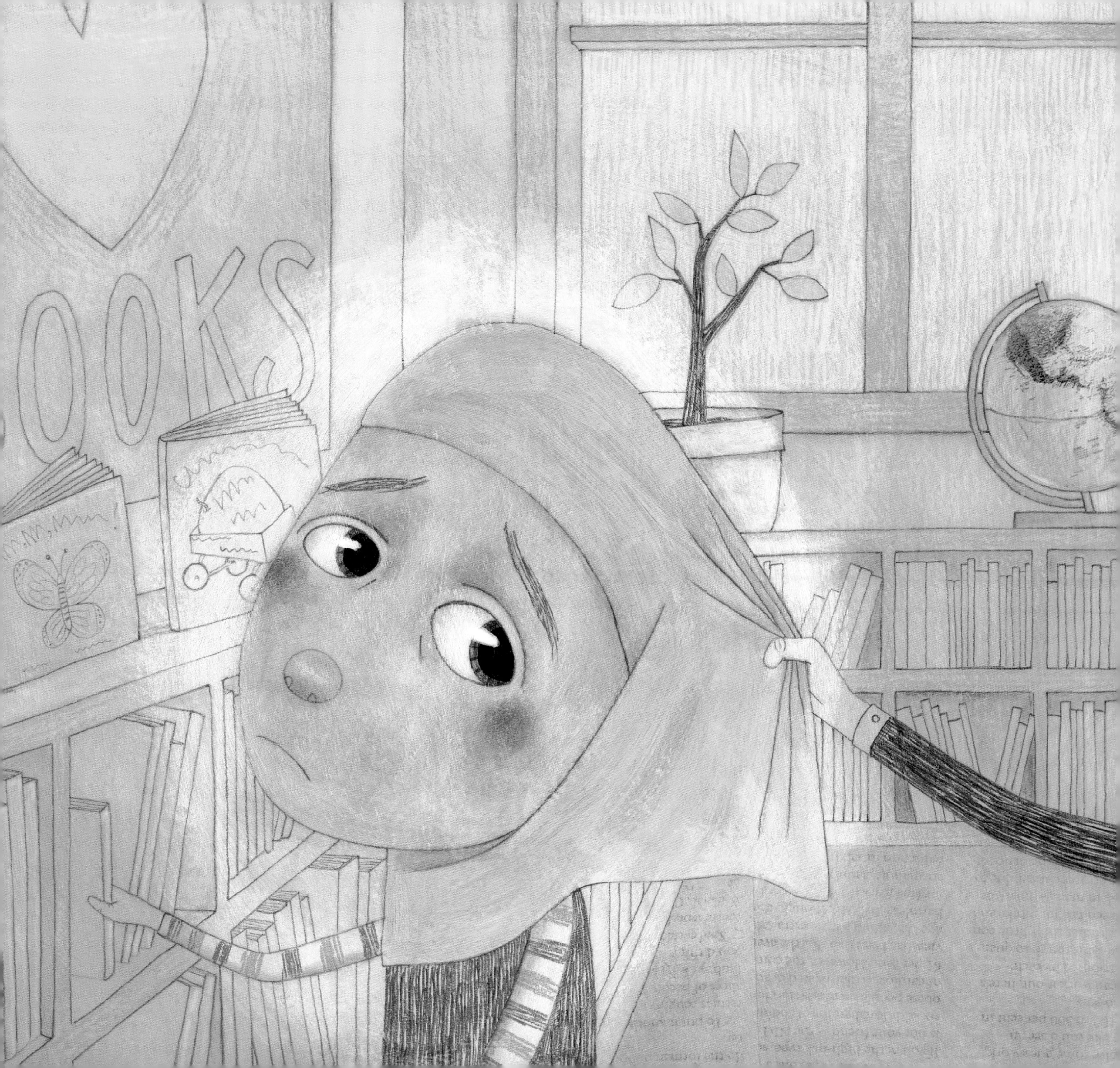
OOKS

Then they went after Liam.
But I can walk –
So I didn't stand up for him.

Then they went after Alexis — she used to be Alex.
But everyone knows my gender —
So I didn't stand up for her.

Then they went after Marvin.

But I'm not fat –

So I didn't stand up for him.

... and I was afraid of standing alone.

But I didn't have to.

We all stood together.

Author's Note

I was inspired to write *I Didn't Stand Up* after reading a poem taped to a teacher's door at the school where I work. The poem was called *First They Came*. No one knows for sure exactly who wrote *First They Came*, but it was made popular by a Protestant Pastor named Martin Niemöller after World War II. The poem talks about the people who were mistreated and even killed by the Nazis, and about how cowardly many Germans and church leaders acted by not speaking up and protecting the innocent victims.

Some targets of the Nazis were Russians, Polish citizens, Jewish people, school children, the very sick, and even the press.

Being a teacher, I see so many forms of bullying - and every one of them breaks my heart. After reading *First They Came*, all I could think about was writing something for children who are mistreated and bullied every day, everywhere. That something became this picture book, *I Didn't Stand Up*.

I think the important question each of us must ask is the same today as it was so many years ago: Who will raise their voice when others are being persecuted?

Will it be you?

The United States Holocaust Memorial Museum in Washington quotes this version of the speech:

First they came for the Socialists, and I did not speak out—
Because I was not a Socialist.
Then they came for the Trade Unionists, and I did not speak out—
Because I was not a Trade Unionist.
Then they came for the Jews, and I did not speak out—
Because I was not a Jew.
Then they came for me—and there was no one left to speak for me.

Pastor Martin Niemöller (1892–1984)

Pastor Martin Niemöller (1892–1984) supported the Nazis at first, but later he had a change of heart and spoke out against them. He became a leader of a group of German ministers who opposed Hitler.

Because of his actions Niemöller was arrested, and in 1937 he was sent to two concentration camps, Sachsenhausen and Dachau. In 1945 the war ended and Niemöller was released. He spent the rest of his life speaking about healing and speaking out against injustice.

Niemöller's work for world peace won him many awards including the Lenin Peace Prize (1967) and the Grand Cross of Merit (1971).

The average student will hear 150,000 putdowns – of himself and others – before graduating from high school. My hope is that all who read this book will take some action to stem the tide of bullying in our schools.

Be the person who speaks up
when someone is being put down

MY PROMISE
If you fall, I will lift you up
If you are lonely, I will be your friend
If you are bullied ...
I WILL STAND UP FOR YOU